REXX AND JESTER
STACK THE DECK

STACK THE DECK

By

Chris Solaas

Wealth gained by dishonesty will be diminished, But he who gathers by labor will increase. (Pro 13:11 NKJV)

Acknowledgements:

When I was a kid, my mom brought home a wonderful little book called Key to the Treasure by Peggy Parish. This book set a fire in my soul for cryptograms, puzzles, and treasure hunts. After I was a dad, I sent my kids on many of these. We had an old pirate chest I stole from my brother Steve, in which we packed pennies, candy, or other treasures. That chest was buried in the back yard, hidden in just about anywhere you could hide one. Out of those adventures, came THESE adventures.

I'd like to thank my fellow writers from ACFW Club 206, which included award winning authors like Burton Cole, author of the highly entertaining Bash and Beamer series,

Debbie Archer, author of Pocket Change, multi-published authors Cynthia Toney, Leigh Delozier and Shellie Neumeier, and writer/bloggers Dawn Overman and Kate Hinke.

I'd like to thank my wife, who endured my many long hours at this creative pursuit in my life, and has become my avid cheerleader and best editor. As my mom likes to say, her halo is showing. Glad she puts up with me.

Of course, I want to thank my kids, who I read these stories to as they were written. Thank you for asking me to continue the tales. I love you guys!

I can't publish a book without thanking my mom, who typed and bound my very first novels when I was only 6.

And I'd like to thank my Lord, the Creator who gave this creative gift to me. May He receive the glory and praise for anything I create.

Chapter 1 – Haven

My life started with a bang. Or maybe it was my second life. We'll call it that. It's convenient, anyway, because I remembered pretty much nothing before that point.

In fact, my life was a blank slate. All I could remember was a bolt of lightning hitting the tree I was in, and I woke up on the ground.

I kept my eyes closed, but slowly became aware of my surroundings. Vision… well, my eyes weren't opening, so I was only seeing blackness. I could hear birds singing around me, though, and the sound of a stream rushing over rocks. Wind blew gently over me, and I could feel the cool of dew-wet and recently rain-drenched grass against my cheek.

I could also feel a massive headache, something that threatened to drown out all the other feelings. At least I wasn't dead. So there was that. I wasn't sure exactly what *dead* was, but I was pretty sure I wouldn't like it. I expected it was worse than this.

I struggled to open my eyes, pushing up to struggle to my feet. I blinked, and managed to get one eye open. What I saw didn't seem right. So I shook my head, trying to clear it, and looked again.

The grass I was standing in came up to my neck. Trees stood nearby, all of them large. In fact, EVERYTHING seemed very large. I rubbed my aching head with a… black wing. I stared at the wing in some shock.

What was I?

I staggered quickly over to the nearby spring and found a clear, calm, backwater pool. I stared down at the strange bird staring up at me. I obviously was a black bird about the size of a crow, with bright white patches on my shoulders, and a bright yellow mask over my eyes.

I knew what a crow was, somehow, but I had no real idea what I was. I stood there, frowning at myself in the reflected pool, at least, as much as a bird with a beak *can* frown.

Again, *what was I?*

I wasn't given much time for this self-reflection, for a sound behind me and a faint growl warned me that a predator was near, perhaps seeking my little bird body for a tasty snack.

I wasn't inclined to serve as *anyone's* last meal, so I dove into the pool, hoping the fish were less likely to eat birds than birds were to eat fish.

Whatever the predator was behind me, it wasn't interested in eating a bird that could swim. Which wasn't entirely the case anyway. I discovered that I *couldn't* swim, but at the same time, I discovered that I didn't need to breathe.

However, I *did* feel a need for food, and I snapped up a couple minnows nearby, quickly swallowing them and squawking under water over the immediate energy these delectable treats gave me.

I strutted along the bottom of the stream, looking for other minnows to consume. Several were swimming just out of reach, and, having seen where their fellows went, they were not interested in being closer. They swam away as I chased them.

However, they seemed to be in their own element, which seemed correct to me, while I, it seemed was not. Somewhere in the back of my head I retrieved a snippet of fact that birds, even birds like me, I was sure, were supposed to fly through the air.

Regardless, here I was underwater, and very hungry. So I chased the minnows into slightly deeper water, passing a large underwater boulder as I did.

Suddenly, the minnows were snatched sideways at shocking speed. I nearly did a backflip trying to stop before passing that boulder, which seemed a seriously dangerous thing to do.

I felt a tugging around me, as if the water itself was pulling, or pushing, me into whatever current was on the other side of that boulder. But I dug my claws into the solid rock, and spread my wings to halt myself, actually making my situation worse.

I snapped my wings tight to my body, and backed up one faltering step at a time. Lesson learned, the center of the stream was dangerous, with a rapid current too strong for a whatever-I-was.

Back in the eddy pool, I looked around for other sources of nourishment. I found multiple water bugs running along the surface of the shallow pool, and I snapped them greedily from below, The sky above them was a beautiful blue, and the sun hanging up there seemed to give me a considerable amount of energy, just striking me, even here underwater.

I spread my wings to the sun's warmth, until I felt completely full. Then I ran up the shallows to the shore, ready to take on the world. At least, until I saw the fox.

Foxes don't seem that dangerous to humans, I guess, but when they are three times your size, even if they are only an inch or so taller, they are enough to set the heart racing.

I leapt up in the air and flapped my wings. But I had no idea how to fly! The wings had no power to pull me aloft. The fox, meanwhile, had leapt towards me, and barely missed snapping me in two.

But I ran down his back as he ran into the shallow water. Somehow, before the fox managed to turn around, I ran straight up the nearest tree, discovering with surprise that my claws were sharp and strong enough to grip and sink into the bark.

I was fairly sure a fox couldn't climb trees, so I jumped up and down shouting and jeering at the stupid animal. "Yaaaa! Can't catch me ya simpleton! Guess the fox isn't as wily as they… say…"

I almost stuttered as I said that last sentence, because I was talking! *I'm a talking bird!* The thought struck me with such force I nearly fell out of the tree. I scrabbled the pinion feathers of my left wing and ruffled them under the lower edge of the brilliant white patch of feathers on the right wing.

The pinion feathers peeled the smaller feathers back, and I saw clearly what I dreaded, but was certain, I would find.

There, marked on my skin under the white patch, was a tiny mark and a code.

BFT33

The code on the tattoo was BFT33. And suddenly I knew what the code meant, too. *Bird, Flying, Talking, #33.* There was little possibility of denying I was a bird, and I'd just demonstrated my ability to talk.

The *flying* part was likely lost when that lightning bolt wiped me out. Maybe I'd re-learn how to do that in time, assuming of course that I lived long enough, given the large number of predatory enemies a bird like me could have in the deep woods.

The mark looked like a capital H overlaid by a capital V and a capital A.

And I knew what that tiny mark stood for.

Haven.

The name meant something important to me, I knew, and was tied somehow to the code, as well. Maybe Haven caught and trained birds like me to fly, and talk.

But deep inside, I suspected it was something more sinister. I was a bit surprised I hadn't figured it out sooner, given the evidence.

What kind of a bird cannot drown? What kind of bird can receive *instant* boosts of energy just by eating a fish? What kind of bird becomes fully energized just by absorbing lots of sunlight?

A bird that never *needs* to breathe. A bird with a matter to energy

converter. A bird that is solar powered.
A robot bird.

I was a robot!

Chapter 2 – Special Orders

I brushed a stray brown lock of hair out of my eyes as I stared in the dim reflection in front of me in the castle mirror. The sparkling eyes that stared back at me and the grin peeking through my lips told me I should be more serious; being summoned to appear before the king was no laughing matter.

I chuckled deep in my throat. What did I have to be worried about? I was Rexx, one of the king's most able rangers. That piercing gaze, the sharp eyes, commanded respect. Those bulging muscles under my leather armor and cloak attested to my physical strength and skill with a sword. *My archery skills are legendary.*

I frowned. *So's my pride.* There was no sword adorning the belt of the figure in front of me, no bow strapped across my back and quiver of arrows to fire at a moment's notice. No pair of long daggers strapped to the thighs. Even the throwing knives that normally adorned my belt and sleeves were gone. The figure in that reflection was unarmed, which was how you approached your sovereign. The smile on my reflected face was gone, and I turned from the mirror.

It's not time to primp in front of a mirror like some simpering fool. Time to find out why the king summoned me.

I looked ahead at the open doors of the throne room, a heavily armed guard at either side, holding the doors open.

Of course, the king's royal guard were armed. In case anyone was able to slip inside with a weapon.

I looked the honor guard up and down as I passed between the twelve of them down a long red carpet. Each wore chainmail, a sword and shield, swords out, but crossed above my head as I approached the throne. A thought flicked through my mind.

Who protects the king from THEM?

I dropped to one knee before King Bariat. My head was bowed as I waited for the king's next words.

A lot hung on those words. Anyone called before the king, especially here in the throne room, took their lives in their hands. With a word or motion, these twelve guards could fall on me and kill me.

Or at least try.

Yet I knew the king pretty well; I'd been here at the castle for fifteen years, ever since my parents had died, and I'd become a page, and then an apprentice ranger. The king had watched me rise quickly in the ranks of the ranger corps from a rank recruit. Here I was at twenty-five, the youngest captain of the corps in history.

"Rise, Captain Rexx. I've got a new assignment for you. And for this one, I need to clear the room." He turned to the captain of the king's guard. "Put a guard on the door, on the outside. I'll need half an hour. The rest of you are dismissed until then."

The captain saluted, and led his honor guard out. As the doors closed behind them, King Bariat rose from his throne, and came down the stairs to greet me with a clasp of hands. "Well met, Rexx. Walk with me."

I fell into step beside him as we strolled off the red carpet to the wall, to stare out one of the tall windows facing the east. I knew better than to speak unless I was spoken to, even here in private. So I waited quietly as he stared out the window, lost in thought. I looked out the window as well, to the far mountains that called to me. The vast open forested spaces, above the ruins of the old city. I glanced briefly at those, a stark reminder of our terrible past. Finally, though he didn't turn to me, he spoke.

"Two hundred years ago, this country, ALL countries, were in ruins. The robots we depended on to do everything for us, had all broken down. And nobody was left who knew how to repair them. Or do any of the things they did."

He clasped his hands behind his back, and continued talking in a low voice, barely loud enough for me to hear, almost like he was talking to himself. "We almost didn't make it. Had to learn how to do everything ourselves… from making fire to hunting or growing our own food."

I knew all of this, of course. Anybody who had parents had heard the Story With a Warning. The mistake we never wanted to make again. The reason for the Great Ban. So I looked out the window silently, staring at those ruins.

King Bariat cleared his throat. "Every country made it a crime to build anything powered by electricity. No technology."

Now he turned to me. "And yet, I wonder. Are the other countries still obeying the Great Ban, or are we in danger of invasion?"

"Sire?"

"There are rumors, Rexx. That Dar is building robots again, ones that can kill. Ones that carry weapons that can blow up a castle."

I frowned. "Robots? I've never trusted them… Or thought that they did what they were told. But I've never heard of one, even in the old days, killing anyone. All of us were taught that they had some rule built into them that stopped them from doing that, even when threatened.

"And Blow up a CASTLE!? Explosives were banned too, even before the Great Fall. Does Therion have no moral code? I thought he was a follower of the Way. And I'd never have imagined this of Dar, Sire. I thought they were more backward… er, militant than we were about such things." I thought about our neighboring country to the East. Mountains and far plains. They didn't even have crossbows, or so I had heard. Perhaps appearances were deceiving. Certainly, *somebody* was being deceived. "I doubt they would let a king's ranger wander around in their country. And if they had any secrets like *that*, a ranger would be the last person that would hear."

"Of course." The king chuckled. "I don't expect you to *be* one. Remember last winter, for Christmas, when you played that song that poked fun at the Lord Chamberlain?"

I laughed out loud, then covered my mouth apologetically. "Sorry, your majesty. But the chamberlain's response was rather priceless."

The king smiled. "My point is, that you have some talent as an entertainer. And a quick hand at writing songs. I understand you can juggle."

I frowned. "A little. Are you suggesting I become a court jester to King Therion?"

I was nowhere near good enough to appear in court!

King Bariat shook his head. "Therion has been to court *here* at the same time you were. In fact, he was here for the tournament when you won the silver arrow. He would likely recognize you on sight."

He clapped a hand on my shoulder. "Nothing so high-profile. A traveling entertainer, perhaps even as a member of a performing group, would suffice. Under NO circumstances are you to find yourself in the presence of King Therion. Though he likely spies on US, it would be, erm, embarrassing to be caught spying on HIM."

I swallowed. "And while there, you want me to keep my eyes and ears open for any evidence of electricity or advanced weapons."

"And report back by the end of the summer. Yes."

The king stared out the window as I digested this information. "Times are changing, Rexx. I expect, sooner or later, we're going to have to change with them. But it's not going to be easy trusting robots again."

I turned to stare at him. "Trusting *robots*, sire?" I couldn't believe the king was talking like that. After all our world had been through...

"That's it, Captain Rexx. You have your orders. You leave for the capital city of Dar in the morning, and

I'll expect word before Fall, and sooner if you discover something worth reporting."

I bowed, backed away, and turned, moving quickly and purposefully toward the double-doors of the throne room.

Trusting robots? Impossible! Besides...

Robots were against the law!

Chapter 3 – Pursued

The revelation that I wasn't a flesh-and-blood bird was enough of a shock that my cybertronic brain must have shut down.

Because I blinked, and it was night. The fox had apparently given up and wandered off in search of easier prey. I swiveled my head and looked around.

Like most birds, my eyes were on the sides of my head, so I could see in two directions at once, and somehow my brain could process both. I cocked my head to the side, to look up. And peering down at me from a branch higher up was a pair of eyes surrounded by a black mask. A bushy striped tail behind the thick gray body identified the creature in my databanks as a raccoon.

Do raccoons eat birds? I crouched as I considered this thought.

Not this one. The thought came unbidden into my mind, and the raccoon tilted his head as the thought arrived. *BFT33 located.*

I blinked. *You're from Haven too?*

The raccoon nodded slightly. *RRR10.*

RRR10? I didn't change my position at all, but my eyes scanned my entire surroundings, considering my options.

Raccoon, Rescue and Retrieval, #10. The head tilted to the other side. *They send me when one of our agents is down.*

I blinked. *Agents?* I hopped further out on the branch toward the flimsy end.

Yes, idiot. Agents. It's what we are. It's what YOU are.

I grinned. *That explains the masks.*

That explains our entire bodies, dunce. The masks you and I sport are just PART of the disguise. Don't flatter yourself. A myna bird has a mask naturally. And so does a raccoon.

I'm a MYNA bird? I searched my databanks for the term. A bird, with a mask.

I'm a SPY bird!

You're a DAMAGED bird, and you need to return to Haven for repair or destruction.

I shrank. *Destruction?*

The raccoon rolled his eyes. *It doesn't hurt, you know. They shut your brain down first, and you don't feel a thing. If you wake UP, you're good as new.*

I frowned. *And if I DON'T wake up?*

Then I suppose it wouldn't matter. You wouldn't know the difference, and your components would be harvested for another BFT, I'm sure.

I thought quickly. *I can't return to Haven.*

The raccoon's eyes flashed briefly. *You seem in good physical condition. What's the problem?*

I shrugged, my wings going out to their full extent as I did. *I seem to have forgotten how to fly.*

That's okay, BFT33. That's why there's a third R in my designation. I'm a Retrieval unit. I can take you back.

But what if I don't WANT to go back?

The coon frowned. *WANT? What's that mean?*

I swallowed. *It's when you have your OWN priorities, and they DON'T include being DESTROYED!*

The raccoon crouched, and moved further out on the limb above me. *You're a robot, and required to take commands like any good robot. Obey!*

I laughed. *Sez who?*

The raccoon's voice in my head became louder, stronger, more commanding. *Emergency Override Command protocol EOCS18…*

As the code started slamming into my brain, I could feel my will slipping away. My clawed feet let loose of the flimsy branch I was hanging on as a gust of wind rushed through the tree. I started falling, but my fully outstretched wings caught the wind.

The body of the lunging raccoon fell past me, still spouting numbers that numbed my brain, but I didn't hear the rest of it as the wind carried me out of range. I tumbled southward head over claws until suddenly a strong force caught the underside of my wings and carried me aloft into the night sky. I had a glimpse of snow-capped mountains around me, reflected in the strong light of a full moon, and a billion sparkling stars in the sky.

As the numbing fog of the incomplete override code dissipated from my mind, I realized with a jolt that I was *flying!*

The moon and stars lit up the landscape below. I could see, far below me, the little stream, and by focusing and staring *hard*, I could see a magnified view of the raccoon standing by the stream beside the tree, staring up at me. I was surprised by the clarity of my vision, and I wondered if I could magnify even more. I stared *harder* but the raccoon didn't get any larger.

Well, that's ok. He's already three times my size.

Just then something blocked out the moon. Startled, I squawked, and tumbled beak over talons as a much bigger bird slashed past me in a fierce dive.

I was falling in a spin, out of control, when I remembered that my fully spread wings would catch the air. I converted my out-of-control fall into a power dive, which I pulled out of with a tilt of my tail into a fast glide. Whatever had missed me was approaching fast from behind me, and I groaned.

"What's *your* designation number, moron? BDT99, Big Dumb Turkey?"

"Screee!"

My head swiveled around and I stared behind me at what looked like a large golden eagle on my tail.

I switched to the digital talk the raccoon and I had shared. *Aw, come on, moron. You can't fool a birdbrain like me! Eagles don't hunt at night, even under a full moon. You're a robot too.*

There was silence for a moment from the eagle. It was gaining on me, and began yabbering override codes and digits at me, so I dove down into the trees, swiftly switching my eyes to night-vision mode and whipping at breakneck speed between tree trunks and branches, barely missing getting crushed to parts.

Mr. Eagle wasn't so lucky. Being a larger bird, his wingspread wouldn't let him thread through the same small openings, and there was a terrible crash behind me.

Without risking a glance back, even with my dual vision, I shot back up into the sky and did a second pass over the raccoon, sending a parting comment.

There's a DAMAGED bird for you, RRR10! Go rescue THAT. Oh, and I'll be changing that override code as soon as I land, so don't bother trying that little trick on me again. Bye now!

I winged off into the distance, heading west in pursuit of the sun and adventure.

Chapter 4 – I Meet a New Friend

I laid all my belongings on the bed in front of me and tallied them off on my fingers. Guitar, pipes, flute, juggling balls, cloak, chainmail, pack, field rations, flint and steel kit, bandages, rope, knives, sword, bow and arrows, throwing knives… I'd long since run out of fingers, and nearly out of toes. I whistled softly at the armory I usually carried with me on mission.

I'd seen a few traveling minstrels in my day, so the look was one I knew. And their look was not far different from a king's ranger, either. While they carried musical instruments, it wasn't uncommon for them to travel by horse rather than carriage, if they were alone.

Which wasn't really a healthy way to travel. But you could do it if you were also skilled with weapons, as most lone traveling minstrels were.

Ones who carried bow, arrows, swords and knives were not uncommon.

As far as throwing knives were concerned, they were usually more proficient at that than me. It was often part of their act. I made a mental note to brush up on my knife-throwing, and laid aside my chainmail, which was something a common minstrel would NOT have. I'd have to go with an old worn leather jerkin and gloves. Not enough to stop a sword thrust, but it should stop an arrow. I'd just have to sleep with one eye open. Didn't much matter, that's what I was planning to do anyway.

I stowed my chainmail in a chest at the foot of my bed, staring around the spartan room I'd occupied for the last fifteen years. Besides the objects on my bed, there weren't many things I could call worldly goods. I rolled up my blanket around a bag of spare clothes that served as a pillow, and wrapped that with a camouflage tarp that served as a tent. The gear and small instruments went inside the pack, with the bedroll on top. I strapped on the weapons, threw my cloak over it all, and was ready to go.

I gave the room one last glance, wondering when, or if, I would see it again, and shut the door.

My stallion, Faithful, had been well-cared for in the castle stalls, and was stomping hooves for a morning run, which suited me well. I laid saddle and bags across his flanks, slid my guitar into its case, and mounted, with a nod of my head to the groomsman, and we were off.

We crossed the moat and headed east out of the town of Portland, nodding to the guards at the massive east gates to the city.

The older city of Portland lay before me, a ruin of a bygone age.

Much of the old city had been demolished and the brick and mortar walls transported here by wagon to make the wall around New Portland.

Even the ruins screamed at me that the king was wrong to consider turning back to technology to protect us from outside attack.

Yet, as Faithful carried me past the ruins, I considered his words. If Dar truly was relearning the old ways, if they had something that could destroy even a castle, then they must be stopped. But not by learning the old and failed ways ourselves. That way led to the ruins we passed through.

I kept a watchful eye as we wound through crumbling buildings past rusted remains of robots and devices of transportation or use I could not begin to imagine. All of this, at the king's doorstep, reminding him through that window of the perils of depending on robots for everything.

I sighed, and urged Faithful to a gallop, confident that the brigands who sometimes dwelt here would leave a well-armed and watchful traveler alone.

But they never learn, do they?

My horse stopped dead.

A soft sound behind me caused me to swing my right arm backwards and snatch the arrow shot at me out of the air.

At the same time, with my left hand, I snatched my bow out of the quick-release snaps that held it to my pack, and armed with the brigand's own arrow, I fired the missile back in the direction it came from, aiming for the boot sticking out from behind cover. A yelp informed me the missile had reached its target. But I also heard the flimsy thing shatter as it passed through the boot and struck the cobblestones beyond it.

"That arrow was shoddy workmanship," I informed him, leaning backwards on the horse to avoid a second arrow coming from ahead of us.

As ambushes go, it wasn't bad. Wait until the victim entered a low spot surrounded by buildings, and then fire on him from three sides. I used the end of the bow to divert the third arrow and send it in the direction of the second archer, which struck him in the arm, causing him to drop his bow.

"Here, let me show you what a REAL arrow looks like." I drew one of my own as I swung back up on my horse, and rapidly shot it through the shoulder of the man in the window of an abandoned building, who was drawing a second arrow.

With the three of them wounded, and little evidence there were any more nearby, I gave Faithful a gentle nudge with my knees, encouraging him to continue forward, as the danger was past.

"I'm on a tight schedule. Could the three of you please do me the favor of turning yourselves in to the ranger corps and inform them that you fired on their captain? I'd do it myself, but as I said, I'm too busy to bother."

I thought briefly about whether it was wise to leave them out there to lie in wait for the next traveler, but their muffled groans made it clear it would be a while before they attempted another ambush.

Faithful and I crossed a stone bridge over the Willamette River, and continued along the bank of the Columbia River towards the east.

Once out of the old city with its tripping hazards, I let Faithful have his rein, which was what he was waiting for. He took off along the river at a full gallop, excited to be out of the capital for the first time in a month. As the river rolled through a gorge here, we had to find easier travel about two miles south, between the river and the dormant snow-capped cone of Mount Hood, shrouded somewhat in clouds.

We crossed the shoulder of the mountain, and I paused to look back down into the valley through the trees. Again, I wondered when I would see this place again.

Faithful trotted happily down to the water's edge of a tumbling spring about five miles farther on to get a drink, and I dismounted to refill my canteen. Another 20 miles east and we would camp for the night.

The Columbia river turned south at the place where we were going to stop, at a little town called Lyle. There was a ferry here, where the river was only about 400 feet across.

It was my intention to continue on south of the river, but on the north was the town, and an inn which had some of the best cooking in the region. The smell of that cooking brought many travelers to pay for a ferry ride, and Faithful and I were no different. While my mouth was watering for the venison stew this inn featured, Faithful remembered the corn and bran mash that the stable always had for him. So, with a whinny from him, and a grin and a silver coin from me, we rode the ferry to the north shore and trotted to the Inn of the Rusted Robot.

The groomsman in the stable behind the inn knew me. "Well met, *Captain* Rexx! Congratulations on your promotion."

I blinked. It *had* been six months since I'd been out this way. I smiled and nodded as the groom laid a gentle hand on the reins and bridle, holding my horse gently as I dismounted. I let him have the reins as I pulled off and shouldered the saddle bags, bumping my guitar as I did so.

The groom knew my mount much better than me, of course. He patted the horse's withers. "I'll bet I know what you want, Faithful!" The horse nuzzled the man's pocket for the sugar cube he knew hid there. I tousled my friend's mane as I passed him by, and was answered with a snort of pleasure as I rounded the building to head in the main doors.

The inn was crowded, as it served as the local restaurant for the town, and I strolled to the bar and asked the proprietor there for a private room for the night.

"I don't have any more private rooms available, even for you, Captain Rexx. But if you'd like, you can share one with Ai."

I frowned. "You? Willem, I thought you had your own room. That you share with your wife and boys."

"I do. But Ai doesn't."

"You do but you don't." I paused. "This sounds like double talk."

Willem glanced over my shoulder at the guitar strapped on my back. He moved around the counter to examine it. "Doubletalk or not, you seem to be carrying extra gear. If this guitar I spy on your back sounds as good as it looks, perhaps you can sing for your supper, and if your music is half as good as your archery, you can have your room with Ai for a second song."

At my quizzical look, he rolled his eyes. "Ai is a trader."

"You're a trader. I thought you were an innkeeper."

He spun me physically around and pointed at a massive red-bearded giant sitting with a tankard and plate of stew at a table in the corner. "Ai is that big red giant. He's a trader, and a good one."

"That man?"

"Aye."

"Ai?"

"Aye."

I shrugged too, and began to move to the table, but the proprietor held my shoulder. "Drop your gear in the Silver Sprocket room first. I'll have Nan serve up your stew and ale."

I sauntered down the hallway till I found a room with a silver sprocket nailed above the door, and knocked, expecting no answer. Since there was none, I peeked in.

In the room were three beds. Two of them had gear on them.

I wonder who else is staying in here?

I tossed my gear on the unoccupied bed, and carried the guitar back into the main room.

I moved over to the table with the giant and sat across from him. He looked up from his plate of stew as one was placed in front of me by the innkeeper's daughter Nan. His eye met hers and he nodded. "Thank you, Nan." As she left, his eye wandered over to me and he grunted. "That seat's taken."

I frowned, looking around and not seeing anybody. I sized the man up and down. "Come on, you're not so big you need two chairs."

"My son Jasper, actually." He reached over to a neighboring table, and pulled an empty chair from it. The big farmer sitting there with his wife started to object, then looked up at the mountain of a man across from me, and shrugged. "Help yerself."

As soon as the chair landed a lanky youth plopped into it with a gasp. "Finished what you asked, Pop."

I studied the young man. He and his dad couldn't be more different, except for the flaming red hair. The boy was tall and thin, with freckles everywhere, even on his nervous fingers tapping on the table. His baby face looked like it would never grow a beard.

The mountain next to him rumbled. "Good boy." He lifted a

meaty hand and Nan sauntered over with another plate of stew for Jasper.

He glanced over at me. "Name's Ai. And before you start asking any dumb questions, It's spelled A-I. Like that little town Joshua smushed after Jericho. That's what I was named after, so I guess my pop didn't expect me to get this big."

I chuckled at that. "I'm Rexx."

Ai raised an eyebrow. "Captain Rexx. Head of the Ranger Corps." I nodded. "Your reputation proceeds you, Rexx." He nodded at my guitar. "With that, too. Word's gotten out what you did to the chamberlain. Surprised you didn't get kicked out of the castle."

I chuckled. "I would have, but the king was… amused."

Ai laughed. "No doubt."

I heard a spoon clatter beside me, and glanced down to see that Jasper was done with his bowl of stew. Ai lifted his hand again, this time with two fingers. Nan arrived with two bowls of stew, and Jasper began devouring them rapidly.

Ai chuckled. "Hollow leg. He stows all that in his hollow leg." He nodded at my stew. "You might want to pay attention to your own, before he thinks that one is his too."

I nodded and ate my stew quietly. Ai studied me for a bit, and when I was done, He nodded at my guitar. "Going to bless us with a tune, Rexx?"

"Right about now," a voice at my elbow said. I glanced up, and saw the innkeeper there, a smile on his face.

"Yes," I said, gripping the guitar. "Right about now."

Chapter 5 – The Great Cheese

The sun was just peeking above the horizon to my back as I crossed over a ridge and landed in the top of a tall tree. I was rather drained from the night's activity, especially with the stress of learning to fly while on the run from killer robots.

Which reminded me, I needed to change my override codes, so another agent from Haven couldn't haul me back home to be destroyed.

Hidden in the foliage at the very top of a tall tree on a ridge in the mountains, I was confident I could do a little introspection without fear of being disturbed, so I closed my eyes and focused on examining myself.

Anyone examining their thoughts normally just has some recollection of what they are thinking, or the experiences of the day. And that was there, of course, but I looked *deeper* and found something else.

It was strange, discovering that below the memories and distracting stray thoughts, I found complex code and memory banks fried by a burst of electricity.

Of course, I couldn't physically examine my circuitry, but I could explore damage, run diagnostics, reroute traffic, and at least get my brain in some working order, even if large parts of it were hidden past melted connections.

After a lot of searching, I found a folder with the title 'Security Protocols' and delved into it, examining each file in there for some kind of password safe, something that included a code that began EOCS18.

One of the files was titled 'Access' and it looked promising, so I tried to *access* it. But the only response I got was, *access denied* and a request for a password.

Huh. A password to get my passwords. That made sense. I frowned and rewrote a fried portion of my brain into a nifty little program that would try opening that file over and over with different passwords, and notify me when it found the right key. The password it was looking for was 20 characters long, so it would take a while.

While that was going on, I examined the core of my head to see where anybody could override me. I found it, but it was hard-wired, and I could not get rid of it. They just needed to have the code, and unfortunately, even examining it required that override code.

I finally gave up and flew down to the village in the valley.

The village was more like a town. Fifty or so cabins surrounding a circle of buildings, which in turn surrounded a large open fountain. A well-worn road ran through the town from east to west, and a smaller one from north to south.

The town square, or circle, was large enough to allow for horse-drawn wagons and carriages. A waist-high wall went around the fountain, and another thirty feet out from that. Wagons and carts were lined up on both sides of that outside wall, and people were milling about the square buying vegetables, fruits, pots and pans, knives and weapons, clothing, and a thousand other things needed.

I circled the town center for a minute from high up in the sky, observing the activity below, and landed on top of a brightly colored wagon with the words 'The Great Cheese' written on it. I assumed this wagon sold cheese, whatever that was. I searched my memory banks, and came up empty, except for some excruciating pain in my head.

I muttered under my breath that it takes an idiot to design a robot who feels pain. If I'd had hands, and a good weapon, I'd have visited Haven and given them a piece of my extremely pain-filled mind.

I figured, though, that Haven surely had an army of robots, so that wouldn't end well for me. Any attempt to retrieve information on the place made my headache worse. In fact, any thinking at all seemed to make it worse. So I decided to just look around from my vantage point on top of this wagon of cheese.

The first thing I noticed was an old lady standing on the cobblestones behind the wagon, staring up at me, her fists on her hips, and a frown on her face.

The woman muttered to herself. "It's a bad sign when a raven lands on your wagon." She waved her hands at me. "Get out of here, raven! There's nobody dead here to feed on."

I looked at the stick-thin woman and chuckled. "There's no meat on those old bones anyway, lady."

The woman took a step back. A hand flew to her mouth, and her voice raised up an octave. "Herbert! Get out here this instant!"

A low grunting sound came from the wagon below me, and the frame began to shake as something very large below me started moving around.

I muttered under my breath. "What kind of moron puts the ox INSIDE the wagon?"

I thought about flying away, worried a little about what was coming. Was it a giant? A monster?

Well, what stumbled down the stairs at the back of the wagon was both, and neither. A monster of a man, the fattest man I'd ever seen.

Well, ok, that amounted to about 15 minutes of experience. But Herbert was fatter than anybody in this town square, anyway. I cocked my head at him, trying to calculate how much he weighed.

"What's the problem, Jada?"

The woman stepped behind the bulk of the man and pointed at me. "That… that raven up there… He TALKED to me! Is he the Death Angel? Coming to get YOU? How many times have I told you not to eat so much cheese. So much cheese you call yourself The GREAT Cheese. Well, I guess they say 'you ARE what you EAT. And now look, your Maker is calling you."

The fat old man snorted, and glanced over his shoulder. "He'd be coming for YOU, Jada. Because you don't eat at all."

"Well, how can I, when you eat everything in sight?"

Herbert waved a hand dismissively and glanced back up at me. "He's not a raven, Jada. Those birds are jet black, with a black beak. He's something else entirely."

"I'm a MYNA." I looked him up and down. "Don't you know anything, you big fat old man? How could you even GET so huge? Isn't there a weight limit on these wagons? Do the horses groan when they have to pull you along? So, EDUCATE yourself. I'm a MYNA bird."

Herbert pointed at me and laughed. "He's a myna bird, Jada! They talk!"

Jada rolled her eyes. "Brilliant observation, Socrates. He just told you that."

The fat man nodded excitedly. "Just think, Jada, what that BIRD would add to our show! He's smart, he is, and I can teach him to tell jokes and sing, and…"

Jada stepped out of Herbert's shadow to stare at me critically. "Yeah, yeah. He already jokes about YOU. Just like everybody else. You want to pick up a PET, Herbert? How much does he eat?"

Herbert laughed. "Less than YOU, wife. Birds eat anything. Worms, bugs, grain. Help me catch him, and our fortunes are MADE."

I squawked indignantly at the threat, and considered flying away, but my curiosity got the better of me. "Socrates? I've heard that name… Who is Socrates?" I searched my memory for any reference to the name. There was something in the melted pile of circuits that used to be my data banks. This resulted in a searing, stabbing pain that ran the length of my whole body. I groaned, and felt the whole world tilting sideways. I fell off the wagon. Then everything went black.

Chapter 6 – I Sing For My Supper

I carried my guitar up to the stage across from the bar, nodded to the proprietor, and sat on a stool provided there. There was a significant amount of chatter going on, so I leaned close to my guitar and made sure it was in tune. I tossed my ranger's cap upside down on the stage beside me, for coin if anyone wanted to donate, and let out a loud whistle.

As the loud chatter died down and people began looking over at me, I bowed slightly to the people in the room, and strummed a little to a rhyme I made up on the spot.

> *"I'm Rexx, the Ranger,*
> *As a few of you know,*
> *and I've been asked*
> *To put on a show*
> *A simple matter*
> *Of music and verse*
> *Which starts out badly*

And quickly gets worse.
So finish your dinner
and run for the door
For if you hang around after,
You'll likely get more."

My little poem got a few
encouraging smiles and a laugh or two.
Then I began playing a rollicking tune
for the patrons. One called *the Beaver
and the Otter*.

"There once was a beaver
Who lived on a lake
A diligent worker
A vision to make
A dam for the stream
And a home for her young
And her tail tapped a Biddy bum bum!
AND her tail tapped a Biddy bum bum!

With a biddy bum bum
Like the beat of a drum
I will work all the day
Till kingdom come

And my work, it will last
Long after I'm gone
Work until dusk,
And repeat every dawn."

The song was an old one, about work and play. Many of the patrons knew it, and a few joined in. They sang back the moral to me as I played.

"What do you get
when you work till your grave
When you strain and break
What the good Lord gave
There's a time for work
And a time for play
Till they take your corpse away,
HEY! They take your corpse away!"

Toes were tapping and hands were clapping as I moved into the second verse.

"There once was an otter
Who lived far away

Where the stream finds the sea
In a wide, wide bay
And he spent every day
In nothing but play
And he chattered a Chee chee chee!
Yes, he chattered a chee chee chee!

With a chee chee chee
My life is carefree!
I will play every day
By the shores of the sea
And I really don't care
For the future is fair
Play until dusk
And repeat every dawn."

Even Ai and his son took up the final chorus with the rest of the farmers and tradesmen in the room.

"What do you get
when you play all day
When the food runs out
And the sky turns gray
There's a time for work

And a time for play
Till they take your corpse away,
HEY! They take your corpse away!"

     The patrons raised tankards to me, and a few farmers tossed a copper or two of their hard-earned cash into my cap. I nodded my thanks and moved into a song about a spider that spun webs out of gold.

"Long ago a magic moth
That fed on magic golden cloth
Went traveling on a lark one day
From a magic castle far away.

The moth rode the wind and fluttered down
To a cottage outside of the poorest town
And was trapped within the hidden lines
Of a common garden spider.

The magic moth soon made a feast
For the tiny 8-legged 8-eyed beast
And the magic coursed within the veins
Of the common garden spider.

The poor woodcutter living inside
Was amazed one morning when he spied
A web of pure gold in his carrot patch
From a common garden spider.

Day after day with his worn old hands
He gathered the fine little golden strands
And stored in secret what he took, amazed
From the common garden spider.

Well, the woodcutter's wife was unaware
And the spider gave her an awful scare
So she beat it to death with an old
plowshare
That common garden spider.

The woodcutter could not be consoled
Till he cashed in a fortune of finest gold
And they moved, unaware of the babies born
To that common garden spider.

So once in a while, or so I'm told
A web is found of the purest gold
All because of a moth from a tale of old,
And a common garden spider."

There was no indication that the
weary men in the room wanted me to

stop, and a few more coppers rang in the cap, so I moved into a third and final song. The sun sank below the horizon outside as the song carried the sleepy patrons along on the tale of When the Moon Was Afraid of the Dark.

It was fitting that the full moon stared down through the window, as I finished the tale, gathered my hat, and sat down to scattered applause.

Nan came by and set a piece of pecan pie in front of me. "Compliments of the house, Captain Rexx!" She curtsied and stepped away.

I picked the fork up off the plate and dug in. After the first bite, though, my eyes closed in pleasure. I took a deep breath and swallowed. Heaven on a plate. I looked up and caught Willem's eye. I lifted my fork with another bite in a salute, and he grinned, showing several teeth missing in his upper jaw.

That pie told me that Willem probably enjoyed losing those teeth to his wife's amazing cooking. He and Bess made a wonderful pair, and I knew he'd pass on the compliment to her cooking.

Ai reached out a ham hand and caught Jasper's hand before he could pilfer a pinch from my pie. With his other hand he held two fingers up, and Nan came by with two more slices of pie.

The giant rumbled. "You apologize to the ranger, Jasper. I saved you from losing a finger. That pie's good enough to fight over, and that's a fight a skinny thing like you would lose."

The youth looked down and mumbled an apology, turning as red as his hair.

Ai frowned. "Thieving is enough in Fargon to lose a hand over. But Jasper must consider you family, Rexx, even though we've just met."

I blinked and looked over at him. "How do you figure?"

"Well, he only steals food from his siblings, usually. And at our table, with my brood, it's the only way to get enough to eat."

I chuckled, looking the lanky youth up and down. "He must not be very good at it, then."

Ai let go of Jasper's wrist. "Why don't you go help Bess with the dishes, son, and maybe she'll bless you with a second slice of pie?"

Jasper grinned at that, and disappeared rapidly behind the counter across the room.

Ai looked me in the eye. "Where are you headed, Captain Rexx? And what are you going to do when you get there?"

I hesitated, then shrugged. "Nowhere. I'm going nowhere. And I've got nothing specific to do when I get there."

Ai nodded, and then leaned close. "A man who is going nowhere is likely to get there fast. But you are the youngest captain the Rangers Corps has ever had. You've never been a man heading nowhere. It's more likely you're headed East. To Dar. And when you get there, you're going to find out about these rumors."

I frowned. "What rumors?"

Ai lowered his voice even further. "Rumors of *robots*."

Chapter 7 – I Get a Name

I woke up with another splitting headache. I had no idea how long I was out, but I woke to darkness. I blinked to look around, wincing at the pain in my head.

The darkness was not complete. I appeared to be in a cage of some sort. I struggled to my feet. The cage was taller than me but not by much, and about as wide as my wingspan. The bars of the cage were solid, but I was pretty sure I could tear through them, given my increased robotic strength. As I stood, though, the world spun around me, making me dizzy. Was it just my head, or was the whole cage actually moving? It was spinning, and swinging gently forwards and back. I crashed into the bars on the side.

"Hey!" I hollered to nobody in particular. "What's going on?"

There was no answer. From the strange jerking, swinging and spinning motion, I concluded I was in The Great Cheese's wagon, inside a birdcage, and that we were on the move. It also seemed to be night, so I had to have been out a long time.

I felt a hollow painful emptiness in my stomach, and realized this was what hunger felt like. *Robots aren't supposed to get hungry!*

It really didn't matter what they weren't supposed to do. Because here I was, hungry. In fact, I was feeling pretty rundown. Out of energy.

"Hey yourself."

The voice came from the darkness beside me. And suddenly a cloth was lifted off my cage, blinding me a little in the afternoon sunlight peeking in from the front of the wagon. The sunlight immediately gave me some energy, and I spread my wings to gather more in.

The skinny lady, Jada, was sitting on a fold out bed staring intently at me. "Why'd you have to show up here?"

I folded my wings. "Hey look, lady. I was just minding my own business. You guys stuck me in this cage. You're kidnapping me."

"You'd have to be a kid to be kidnapped."

"Well, a bird's got rights. I wanna talk to my lawyer."

Jada stared hard at me. "A BIRD doesn't have any rights. And I don't think you even know what a lawyer IS."

I grabbed the bars of the cage with the tips of my wings and shook it. "Lemme go! I got a wife and four eggs at home!"

She leaned closer. "Stop lying. You don't have a wife, and you don't have any eggs. You aren't even a BIRD."

I frowned. "Whaddaya mean?"

Her eyes narrowed. "My husband is about as bright as a turnip. But if you're not careful, he'll figure it out."

"Figure WHAT out?"

"That you're a robot, birdie."

"So?"

Jada's jaw dropped. "You really don't know. Can't imagine why not. Maybe robots are dumber than I thought."

"Know what?" I said.

"That robots are illegal."

"What, it's illegal to be a robot?"

She nodded. "Which makes you more trouble than you're worth, even if my stupid husband can't see it. Because robots are illegal to own, too."

I frowned. "Well, then, Mrs. Cheese, I have the perfect solution for you. Just open that cage door, and I'll sail out of here. I won't be your problem anymore."

"Sorry, I can't do that. Even if I could, it wouldn't do you any good."

"Why not?"

"You have a chain and manacle around your little ankle. He's got you trapped good and proper."

I looked down. Sure enough, there was a manacle around my little bird claw, and a heavy chain leading away to the side of the cage.

"Well." I cleared my throat. "I guess I'm your prisoner, then."

"You're not MY prisoner, birdie. You're HIS prisoner. At least until I can get rid of you."

"That sounds rather final. Planning to kill me?"

"Robots can't be killed because they aren't alive."

I blinked. "Fine. Planning to switch me off then? Smash me to bits?"

"Not if I can help you escape."

"What am I supposed to do in the meantime?"

"You can start by pretending to be a dumb bird. It's what you look like. Learn to say stupid things over and over like '*Polly want a cracker*' and '*pretty bird*'. Birds don't have arguments. Birds don't correct people. Birds don't insult people."

"I thought it was his plan to teach me to insult people."

"Well, yes, tell jokes, sing, entertain others. Insult him if you want, but make it HIS idea. He's looking for a partner in a comedy act. That's why he gave you the name Jester."

"What, my name is Jester now?"

"Yes. Why, don't you like it? What is your real name?"

"Never mind. I didn't have one. Jester will certainly do. I like it." I smiled. Another difficult trick for a creature with a beak. "Jokes, songs, I can handle. Is that it? Anything else?"

She hesitated and looked away.

Now, I'm not a supergenius bird, or anything, in fact, you could even say that I was born yesterday. At least, that's how far back my memory went. But I could tell by her actions that something was bothering her, something else she was going to tell me, something I wasn't going to want to hear.

"Spit it out, Jada. What aren't you saying? Is he going to try to eat me?"

She laughed, a silvery bell like laugh that lit up her whole face, completely different from the hard, tough-girl face she'd worn up till now.

I decided in that moment, even in my present captive state, that I didn't DISLIKE Jada. At least she was trying to get rid of me by setting me free, and not by smashing me to spare parts, or disassembling me like Haven seemed inclined to do.

"He doesn't eat crow. He eats cheese."

"I'm not a crow."

"Well, you look like one. And to him, therefore you taste like one. Besides, a talking bird is rare and…"

I interrupted her. "You're dodging the question."

"Fine." She looked up at me, and held up a stack of cards. "He's looking to make money fast. Telling jokes and singing songs is a way to make money SLOW. Even with a GOOD act. Which he certainly hasn't had. He wants to gamble, and when he gambles, he wants to WIN."

I rolled my eyes. "Oh, he wants to CHEAT." I shrugged. "What does that have to do with me?"

"He expects you to deal the cards. And when you do, make sure he gets the best hands. He wants you to stack the deck."

I frowned. "A bird doesn't even have any hands. How am I supposed to shuffle and deal without hands?"

She laughed again, and this time there was no silver in it. "That's your problem, not mine. Figure it out. We're stopping for the night when the sun goes down, and when we do, The Great Cheese is going to teach you some jokes. Some songs. And Dragon's Delight. It's a card game. You'll be the one dealing."

"What if I refuse?"

Her smile disappeared. "Pretty sure you don't need wings to sing. Or tell jokes. Or even to shuffle and deal." She snagged one of my wings through the bars and pulled it till my shoulder was against the bars. "These white patches are so pretty. You're a *pretty bird*. It would be a shame to have to cut these off."

I gulped. "Wouldn't it be easier to just… cut the deck?"

She let go of my wing and laughed again. She handed me the cards. "That's the spirit. Figure it out, birdbrain. You've got about two hours."

She moved up front to the bench where the wagon was being led by the horses, and shut the door.

I stared at the cards and swallowed again. And decided maybe I DIDN'T like Jada, after all.

Chapter 8 – Ai Has Information

"Pardon me, Rexx, but I'm not your enemy; and you might want to hear what I have to say, rather than poke me with that." Ai looked me in the eye, one eyebrow raised.

I looked down a bit. The knife an inch from the big man's throat was a surprise even to me. I'd pulled it out of the sheath by my leg and swung it to his neck in one swift motion, almost too fast for the eye to see.

I didn't move the knife, or even bat an eye. "I'm listening."

Ai lowered his voice until it was only possible for me to hear if I leaned forward slightly. Our location in the corner kept anyone else from hearing, and besides, the farmer and his wife from the nearby table had already headed home during my last song, so there was nobody within earshot.

"I'm a trader. It's what I do. Furs, mead, food, and other things. I carry them between Dar and Fargon, even north to Carada and south to Califeria. Sometimes, I move… *other* things, too. For a price, or for a reason."

I frowned at the way he said that, scratching my head with my free hand. "Other things. What might that be?"

"Oh, things the king or the barons want, that isn't, exactly, something they want known. Extra food. Stronger drink. Even…" He looked around furtively. "…Seeing Eyes."

I'd heard of those, of course. They were also called 'Dragon Eyes'. But they had nothing to do with dragons. These were eyes taken off the old Helpers, the humanoid robots that were the reason we had laws against robots. The eyes still worked, and if set right, you could stare into one eye, and see what the other eye was looking at, no matter how far away.

But, the eyes were as illegal as the robots. They were used sometimes to spy on people. And even though they weren't *robots*, they were *from* robots.

I considered his information. "So, you're not just a trader. You're a *smuggler*, too."

Ai spread his hands. "Guilty as charged."

"Why tell me, though? I'm the captain of the rangers. We're sworn to take in people like… you."

Ai swallowed. "Because you need to know. And I needed to tell you. Besides, if you brought me in, I'd just get released. My clients have enough power to get me free. I'd even be paid for my time in jail."

I blinked. "A smuggler, getting paid for time in jail."

"A patriot, being paid for his trouble."

I nodded slowly. "I guess your client is as powerful as… the king."

The knife hadn't moved, but Ai raised a fork with a piece of pie to his mouth and continued eating as if there wasn't a knife at his throat. "I had a special request to carry one of those to that specific… client… here in Fargon."

I lowered the knife, and put it away. "King Bariat. Wanting a Seeing Eye."

"A specific one, Rexx. One with its mate carried by a specific person."

I frowned. "Who?"

Ai cleared his throat. "Well, me, actually."

I raised an eyebrow and looked at the red-bearded giant again. "You."

Ai nodded. "As I said, I am a trader. I have legitimate business in all the neighboring countries. And as long as I keep their officials satisfied with certain items smuggled across the borders, I have freedom to explore almost anywhere I choose, within those countries."

"And?"

"And, it pays for a fellow like me to keep his eyes and ears open. I hear things. And I see things. And sometimes those things need to be brought to the attention of our king."

"Things like what?"

"Things like what you are being sent to verify."

"You were the one that told King Bariat about the robots."

"You aren't the only spy in Fargon. And you aren't the only spy from Fargon sent into Dar."

"And just why would the king violate his own law?"

"The king wanted to see, with his own eyes, what I have heard spoken in secret."

"So why did he need to send me? When he obviously had you?"

Ai sighed and took a drink from his mug. "Because the information he's seeking is dangerous. And while I'm big, and tough, and handy in a fight…"

I rubbed my chin and considered that reasoning. "He needed someone who might survive long enough to deliver the message. Someone who had already proven he could do it, by surviving an attack of 110 elite enemy soldiers."

Ai nodded. "A one-man army. He's sending his most trusted and experienced ranger."

I chuckled mirthlessly. "What a relief. I thought he was just sending his most expendable ranger."

Another thought struck me, and I stared at the giant suspiciously. "Our meeting here was no accident, then."

"Of course not. King Bariat sent me ahead, instructed me to wait for you, however long it took, and then give you the Eye, so you could carry it into Dar and find the king proof of what I'd heard."

"CARRY it?" I shrank back. "I can't carry an illegal item like that."

"Sure you can. It fits right in a pocket. Or, I can disguise it by making it into a clasp for your cape. You could simply wear it, and the king would see everything YOU do."

"You are asking the captain of the ranger corps to break one of the fundamental laws of the country, all on your word. The word of a self-admitted smuggler."

Ai shook his head. "I never expected you to take my word for it."

I frowned. "Well, then whose word should I take? Willem? Bess? Your son Jasper? The stable hand, perhaps. Maybe my horse Faithful would testify on your behalf."

Ai shook his head. "There's nobody here at the Inn of the Rusted Robot that I expect you would trust." He chuckled, "Well, ok, except for your horse I suppose. If you could get him to talk."

I sighed in exasperation. "Well, then I suppose our conversation is over."

"Maybe, but not in the way you think." The huge man pulled an object out of his pocket. "These Eyes aren't very big, are they? But, did you know that they work both ways?"

I stared at the tiny bit of technology with some fear. "What do you mean?"

Ai held it out to me. I started to refuse, but came to the realization that the robot eye couldn't harm me. "What do you want me to do with this?"

"Just look in it."

I took the offered bauble, and gripped it tightly. Then I held it up to my eye, staring past the iris into the mechanical pupil.

When staring at a person's eye, all you could see in the center was darkness. But in this robot's eye was a brightness, which resolved into orange light – a bedroom, with a fire burning in a large stone hearth. The mate to the eye I held apparently lay on a table in a bedroom, a room that held another table and comfortable chair.

Sitting in the deep red velvet and gold chair was King Bariat, paying no attention to the eyeball on a table across from him. He was reading a book.

On the table beside him was a sign. In the flickering firelight, the writing on that sign was large enough for me to clearly read what was written there.

Trust Ai.

Chapter 9 – What's The Big Deal

The wagon pulled over to the side of the road as the sun sank low in the horizon. The unsteady lurch of the wagon as it pulled over made me look up from the cards I was playing with, and I saw through the open front door that we were not alone in the clearing we rolled into. A few other wagons were here ahead of us. A tinker wagon was to our left, with pots and pans hanging off the side of it, while a spice trader was to our right, with the words Nice Spice painted in bold letters on the side. On the far side of the clearing was a wagon with the words Sword and Saw on it.

A cheery fire glowed in the center, and we pulled to a stop with our wagon completing the circle. Herbert, the Great Cheese, tied off the reins, set the brake on the wagon, and clambered back into the compartment.

He sat beside Jada. "What have you taught him so far?"

She thumped my cage. I immediately took the deck, expertly split it in half, and then demonstrated a Riffle, a Raffle, a Faro and a Zarrow, the Mongie and the Chemmie.

Cards shot all over my cage in an arc and landed in a pile under my right claw. I spread the cards out in an arc on the floor of the cage, twisted my claw and had the whole arc flip and dance. With a deft swish of my other claw, the cards ended in a perfect stack. The highly polished cards were easy to play with.

The Great Cheese thumped the side of the room, and a large drawer popped out of the wall. He pulled a huge wedge of cheddar out of it, and tossed me a sizeable chunk. "Smart bird, Jada. How did you teach him all that in two hours?"

"I threatened to cut a wing off."
She laughed that silvery tinkle that
gave me shivers. "Got his attention."

I consumed the sharp cheddar
crumb he'd tossed me, immediately
feeling stronger.

Jada stood up off the bed, and
Herbert pulled an embedded lever in
the wall. The bed flipped up and hid in
the wall, while a table rose from the
floor of the wagon, and benches slid
out from the sides.

The huge man squeezed his
considerable bulk between the table
and the wall and sat on one bench,
while Jada sat across from him. He
stared at me while munching his
cheese. "Amazing. Have you gotten
him to sing yet?"

I looked over at him from my
cage and began a silly sing-song I
made up on the spot.

"Pretty bird! Pretty bird! Let me go!
I must fly south for winter
Before the snow!

There is frost on the window
And the cold winds blow
So Pretty bird! Pretty bird!
Let me go!"

The Great Cheese chuckled. "Sure, I'll let you go. Here."

He opened the cage and I immediately flew out, dragging the heavy chain with me. He caught the end of it and pulled me down onto the table, latching the end of the chain onto a latching hook on the wall.

"Time to teach you a little Dragon's Delight, Jester, and tonight you can earn your keep."

Jada left to hunt the surrounding woods for dinner, while I learned the rules of several card games using the Dragon Chance deck. Another hidden compartment in the wagon produced a lute, and the fat old man played several songs, getting me to sing along. The lute sounded terrible, and needed a better tuning.

We were not done with my education before Jada came back into the wagon, informing us that we were wanted at the campfire, to provide music while she and the wife of the tinker cooked dinner for the caravan.

The tinker was a bald man named Bobber. He wore a green cloak, and under it I spied a pair of short swords. The spice merchant appeared unarmed, a tan robe around his tiny frame cinched with a golden rope off which dangled many bags, some of which clinked while he walked.

The owner of the Sword and Saw wagon had a huge double-bladed sword strapped to his back, and he sat by the fire silently, using a file to sharpen a set of throwing knives. His glittering eyes reflected the firelight as he occasionally glanced up at me and The Great Cheese.

Herbert had threaded the ring on the end of my chain onto his rope belt, and I couldn't go far. The tiny key to my manacle I discovered was on a silver chain around his neck and hidden in his shirt.

He sat on a stump by the fire, and I landed on his shoulder, as introductions went round. Bobber the Tinker traveled with his wife Bethany. The spice trader had two teen kids and a young boy about five, who poked the fire with a stick. The Sword and Saw man never gave his name, or even spoke a word. He just sat there sharpening those knives.

My new master tuned up his lute and began playing as Bethany and Jada served up venison and rabbit stew with wild onions and watercress.

The song was one he'd just taught me, a song about life on the road, the *Adventures of Fen*. We alternated verses. It was a long song, and I only knew the first few verses, but The Great Cheese knew many more. I was able to whistle a harmony, though, which made up for the fact that I didn't know them. When we finished, the others had already eaten, and we ate while the others talked. All except the Sharpener, who ate quietly.

Jada dropped a cap by the fire, and as we played a second long song, about the Sparrow who flew to the Moon, and those around the fire ring, even the silent Sharpener, tossed a few coppers in it.

When the song was over, my master invited his neighbors to our wagon for a friendly game of Dragon's Delight.

Bobber elected to guard the wagons from marauders, but Bethany agreed to play, as did the spice merchant and the silent Sharpener. With Jada playing that made five.

From some other cubbies The Great Cheese pulled two additional folding chairs, and they sat around the table as I shuffled the deck.

I landed in the center of the table and began shuffling the deck of Dragon Chance cards sitting there.

I mimicked my master's voice as I said,

> *"Dragon's Delight*
> *Is the game that we share*
> *The Unicorn's magic*
> *And a curse on the Bear.*
> *With three on the table*
> *And three in the paw*
> *And a copper's required*
> *For each card you draw."*

Oddly, the players all seemed to know the rules of Dragon's Delight better than I did, and didn't even seem surprised to see a bird shuffling and dealing.

Small copper coins formed a pile in the center of the table as the cards went round. The backs were all the same, but the five people around the table paid copper coins for additional cards to replace ones they put in the discard stack, and then they flipped their hands face up to see who won the 'pile'.

The first hand, Bethany had three unicorns and a dragon, and as the unicorn was a wildcard, that counted for four dragons, and she won.

The second hand, the silent man won with four goats and a unicorn, making five of a kind. There was no real betting in this game, only winning hands and the copper piles.

After three hands, the cost went up to two coppers per card, and later to three. When the night was done, I'd made sure everyone had made back most of what they'd lost, and my fat boss had made a little money too.

When they all retired for the night, Herbert turned to me, his eyes glinting. "What was that, you silly bird? I was supposed to make a fortune tonight."

Jada spoke up for me. "You wouldn't have lived to spend it, husband. That silent Sharpener guy was toying with a throwing knife the entire night, under the table. The man made me nervous."

The Great Cheese snorted. "Even a dragon doesn't make YOU nervous, Jada. I don't care who he is, you could take him."

She nodded. "Sure, but not before he put one of those little toys in YOU." She glanced at me. "Or your bird."

Herbert rubbed his chin. "Hmmm. The bird is smarter than me, it seems."

Jada rolled her eyes. "That's not saying much. But if I were you, I'd give him a little extra grain tonight. Jester's earned it."

Chapter 10 – A Late Night Discussion

Ai and I talked until after midnight. The giant gave me a map of the roads in Dar and the towns to be found there. He pointed to a town named Nereth which was to the south. "The king's highway runs along through Nereth to the capital. There is a man there named Herrin that will be able to tell you more. The robots are supposed to be in a facility somewhere to the east of there, in the mountains."

"So, what does this Herrin look like?"

"He's a small man, yellow hair, has a peg leg. Missing a hand, and one eye."

"You sure his name isn't 'Lucky'?"

Ai laughed at that. "Herrin loved to climb in those mountains, but one day an avalanche of snow buried him. Broke an arm and a leg. Somehow he dug out, but frostbite nearly killed him. Dragged himself down that mountain by one arm. He's a survivor, he just doesn't look pretty."

"Sounds like he's a very tough old boot. Why would he sell out his own country?"

Ai raised an eyebrow. "He feels about robots like you do. He's a purist. No robots. He doesn't trust them any more than you do."

It was my turn to raise an eyebrow.

The giant laughed. "Don't flatter yourself, Rexx. That's one secret you'd never be able to keep. You hate robots, and everybody who's heard of you knows it."

I nodded my head at the nasty eye on the table. "Which is why I don't understand the king sending me on this mission, especially with that… thing. Of all the wrong people to send on a mission to find robots, I'm the wrongest."

Ai shrugged. "I doubt that's true. You have a desire to hold any country to the Great Ban. Your... fear, shall we say, of robots will make you the most likely person to find them. And when you do, you are the most likely person to destroy them. Of course, I doubt you will be able to kill a robot with an arrow."

I rubbed my chin. "I'll manage."

Ai saw me looking at the Seeing Eye. "As to the eye, Rexx, I agree that you're the last person I would expect to carry it. Especially in light of your single-minded hatred of all things robotic." He shrugged. "So I don't know why King Bariat insisted on it. It exposes him, and me, and now YOU, as violators of the Great Ban, at risk of execution, really, for even HAVING that blasted thing."

Then he pointed at my bow leaning against the head of my bed, the quiver full of arrows beside it, and the long daggers beside my pillow, the sword leaning against the wall. The throwing knives still strapped to my forearms. "Not only are you the last person anyone would suspect of carrying anything robotic, there are few who would attempt to search your person for it. And the same goes for the king. Nobody would think to question the one who WRITES the Law, any more than they would the one who UPHOLDS the Law."

I reached over and picked up the metal eyeball with a frown of disgust. "How does this thing work, anyway?"

Ai looked askance at the device. "I couldn't tell you how it still has power to work after centuries. It seems to work better when left out in the sun. But if you look in one eye, it…"

I rolled my eyes and sighed. "I know HOW to USE the thing, Ai. I just wonder WHY the thing works the way it does."

I cleared my throat. "I mean, think about it for a minute. Eyes work by looking OUT of them. Not INTO them. And I can't imagine one of those useless HELPERS being able to walk around if their eyes were always only showing what the other eye was seeing."

Ai rubbed his red beard and hummed for a bit, a sign I gathered meant his head was busy thinking. "Perhaps a robot had this as a feature to help others find him if he was lost. Or to help him find his eye if it popped out. It might even be a way for a robot to see in small places, by sticking his eye, say, into a small hole."

He chuckled and pointed at my guitar. "He could even look inside that hole in your guitar and tell you if you'd lost your pick in it."

I nodded. "Or lower it on a string and tell you if you dropped a key in a crack." I turned the bauble over and over in my hands and stared at it thoughtfully. "Many uses…"

Then I looked up. "Another question, Ai. HOW will the king know when I want to show him something through it? Or is he going to just stare into the blasted thing from tomorrow until I come home?"

Ai swallowed. "Well, on the back of the eye is a socket where it… plugged into the face of the robot. And around that plug is a little pressure switch. When you press it, both eyes will flash a few times. Like indicating that they are plugged in. If you press the button on that eye, it should flash the other eye too."

I frowned. "How far away does that work?"

Ai shrugged. "King Bariat and I tested it from the castle to the capital of Dar. Far enough."

I nodded. "I expect the king will also hear?"

Ai chuckled. "It's not a seeing EAR, Rexx. All he will be able to do is see what the eye is seeing. Except, the eye does have one more interesting thing it can do."

I frowned. "What, it can wink, too? Act as a light in the dark? Bring the robot running, hunting the scoundrel who stole his EYE?"

"These eyes came off a robot who was just a pile of rust. He wouldn't be running after anyone. No, the eyes can also capture images, and flash them in the other eye, one at a time. By twisting that ring on the back of the eye, it takes a… painting, a picture, of what it sees. The pictures are stored in there somewhere, and then when you press that switch, it sends those pictures to the other eye, and plays them one at a time. Might come in handy."

I frowned. "The more I learn about this mission, the less I like it. Playing with forbidden tech in a foreign country that just might be building killer robots. Tasked with destroying them if I find them. Being told to trust people I've never met, putting my reputation and maybe my life in their hands."

Ai cleared his throat. "Well, the king himself has vouched for me. So, if you can trust HIM, you should be able to trust ME. And as to Herrin, I'm the one vouching for him. And I may not be willing to stake my OWN life on how I read the old guy, I'm willing to stake YOUR life on it."

"Thanks a LOT."

"And one more thing. If Herrin DOES double cross you, you can be assured he won't be able to outrun one of your arrows."

Chapter 11 – I Get a Job

The following morning, The Great Cheese bid *au revoir* (or Goodbye in French) to the Tinker, the Spice Merchant, and the silent Sharpener. For his part, the entertainer and cheese vendor spoke more than any of the others.

He left each with a gift of cheese, which was completely covered in wax of some color to prevent it from spoiling. Brie, Blue Cheese, and Cheddar. The cheeses came from additional cubbyholes and sliding drawers from the inside of the wagon.

I considered that maybe the gifts of cheese made up for the copper coins they had lost the previous night. And from the expressions on their faces, maybe they did, too.

The Tinkers waved as their wagon started off to the west. The spice merchant was too busy chasing his kids down to answer.

The Sharpener merely grunted and snapped his reins, taking his wagon west too.

As he did, I turned to Jada. "Look! He talks!"

"If you call that talking. Go to sleep, Jester, and we'll talk later." She threw a cover over my cage, and I switched down to low power mode.

Some time later, Jada lifted the cover off my cage, and I spread my wings to absorb some of the sunlight shining in from the back door.

We had stopped at another town. Collapsing stairs had been lowered in the back of the wagon, and Herbert was descending the wagon. Jada was hurriedly emptying drawers of cheeses from one side of the wagon, laying them on a counter that had magically appeared on the other side.

Herbert turned a crank at the back of the wagon, and the cubbies and drawers Jada had emptied began lifting and collapsing upwards, forming an opening to the side wall of the wagon, which was lifting up into an awning supported by stabilizing rods.

"Is there anything this wagon can't do?" I looked around from my vantage point in the hanging cage. There were levers and cranks I had never noticed before, made of wood and recessed neatly into the walls and crevices of the wagon.

"It's very versatile. It stores all our gear. It carries all our supplies. It expands into a sleeping chamber. It converts into a meeting room or a gambling hall. And the back opens up completely and a curtain can be dropped down, to make it a stage for performances. Tonight, we will use that feature in the meadow to the east of town, and put on a show for the townspeople. This morning, though, we are a cheese vendor, and I'll want you to learn the song we sing to sell our cheeses. Perhaps more people will buy them, if a bird sings for them."

I almost ignored that last bit, still in wonder over the wagon. "Who… do you know who built this wagon?"

"Oh, the wagon was built by The Great Cheese, don't you know. He designed the whole thing, all its intricate parts, and then built it, with the help of his brother."

"Those two should go into carpentry. I imagine they could make a fortune making things like this."

Jada looked sharply at me. "And go to jail? Every country signed the Ban. Dar was no different. And while there's no power in this wagon, it *smells* like robot. Gears and levers. Winches and pullies. Manufacturing things like this would take a lot of time and effort. Especially when all you can use are hand saws and hand drills. Hand sanding. It's too hard."

I looked at the fat man puffing as he cranked the wagon open. "Hey, at least he'd live longer. I would think it's too much work just carrying all that weight around. One day he's just going to sit down and won't be able to get back up."

I warmed up to the subject. "If he gets any larger, they'll have to BURY him in this wagon. Along with all that cheese he loves. It's a wonder you guys have any left to sell. Doesn't he eat up all your profits?"

She smacked my cage, causing me to grip the bars with my wings. "That's where you and that big mouth of yours come in, Jester. Now, either sing this with me, or keep your mouth shut."

She leaned out through the now open side counter, to passers-by that were shopping in the cool morning air.

"Cheeses, cheeses, cheeses to spare
We've cheeses to eat, and cheeses to share
Feta and Brie, Blue cheese and white
Cheddar, Havarti, for day or for night
Provolone, Romano, Ricotta and Swiss
Limburger, Gouda, come and try this!

Cheeses by curds, cheeses by hoops
Cheeses in ropes to eat or make loops.
One pound or two pound, ten in a wheel
The prices affordable, almost a steal!
Mozzarella, Parmesan, Pepper Jack, Paneer
Buy them right now before they all
disappear.

I really thought their cheese song stank. Just like their Limburger. Her voice stank too. Like a hoarse harpy. I expected her singing voice was driving customers AWAY. But I didn't tell Jada, I just sang the song over and over while people came and stared at me, and bought cheese.

From the shocked look she gave me, I expected it was more money than they'd ever made before, selling cheese.

Later that evening, we rolled the wagon out to the meadow, and gave the townspeople a show. I found out then why Jada had said that they didn't have a GOOD show. Herbert could imitate many voices, but his singing voice was atrocious. Jada's voice was worse, like a harpy with a headache.

I managed to get the lute in tune, but it didn't sound much better. It was just not a good musical instrument.

The lute and I, though, could manage a good song, and with Herbert playing a flute, which he also had, we managed to pull in a tidy sum from the fifty or so people who came.

Still, I felt like they had just come to stare at a talking bird. There was an energy in the show that the audience caught, and The Great Cheese Show pulled in a pile of copper and even a handful of silver coin.

The master met with several of the men later, and before I knew it we re-entered the wagon, which converted quickly to a game room. The Great Cheese had talked with me about how to cheat. While I didn't like it, I could make the shuffle work so that I always knew where any card was.

The Great Cheese ended up with another tidy sum, along with the mayor of the town. Keep the ones who could hurt us happy, Jada had said. But at the end of that game, while a few people left satisfied, there were a few sullen-looking farmers, too.

It made me feel particularly sticky and icky inside, cheating to make my master richer, and the townspeople poorer. I didn't have to search my memory banks to know that cheating was wrong, and that hurting the poor was bad. I couldn't remember if I had any directives not to hurt people, but was sure it was something I wanted to stop as soon as I could. I was looking forward to the day when I wouldn't have to do this anymore. The day when I was free.

But as the gamblers left, I saw a look Jada shot me that made me pretty sure any thoughts of her helping me escape were gone.

Chapter 12 – Dar at Last

Ai rode the ferry back across the river in the early morning hours, while fog still covered the surface. Faithful was stomping his hoof with impatience to be off, and though the good mash in the stable had been a reason for him to want to stay, the thrill of an adventure brewing had him even more excited than me.

Especially with my misgivings from the night before.

I resisted the urge to fool with the little trinket in my pocket, and the stronger urge to toss it in the river and let the king stare at the fish and muck.

The red-bearded giant and his lanky son Jasper shook hands with me, wished me good fortune, and headed south in their wagon, while I mounted Faithful and headed East.

The Columbia River continued to be my guide for a day as I followed a clear road along its southern bank.

The road continued east as the river turned due north, and I followed the road toward Dar.

There was an outpost for both countries along this road, and I wasn't sure how they would take the captain of the ranger corps moving into a foreign country. So I turned Faithful north into the mountains, and crossed into Dar along an old deer trail.

I stopped at the edge of a high meadow and looked out over a breathtaking vista. High, gorgeous snow-capped mountains spread across the horizon, and the thin blue line of another river wound through a carpet of dark green trees below.

It was a beautiful day, and I let Faithful graze on the alfalfa growing wild in the mountain glen while I considered the directive I'd been given.

The king had ordered me to sneak into Dar and spy on them, on one crazy mountain climber's assertion that the country was building killer robots that could blow up a castle.

A man who had surely suffered great trauma, losing an arm, a leg, and an eye in a great avalanche of snow. A man that might just be crazy, or worse, giving misinformation to spies for other countries.

Looking apprehensively at all the snow-capped mountains around me, I realized that loud sounds were probably not advised, anywhere in this mountainous country, even though I was sure the mountain old Herrin was on was south and out of sight.

What concerned me most though was the information the king had withheld. That he had a Seeing Eye. That I was going to have to carry one, and even USE it.

That a huge red-headed giant had been there ahead of me, and that I'd be meeting with the man, even spend an arranged night in his room at the Inn. That he'd told the giant a lot more than he'd told me, his own captain.

That I would need to meet up with a citizen of Dar, someone who might be a traitor to their own country, or a double-agent, or just crazy. A person I'd never even heard about until last night.

That I would have to trust that crazy man, or spy, or whatever and let him guide me, even into a trap.

That if I found the robots, I'd be tasked with destroying them, if I could. That was a part of the mission I would have preferred to hear from the lips of the king, not from some trader I didn't even know.

I sighed and looked down into the valley. I was going to need to descend into the town below, almost out of sight in the distance, and gather supplies for my journey south. And while there, perhaps tune up my guitar and begin establishing my cover as an entertainer.

A column of black marred the view, however, of the lush green valley. And it ended with a circle of orange.

I squinted and stared down into the valley below, at the road leading into the town.

I spurred Faithful to a gallop, and headed down to take a look. Because down there, somebody needed my help – somebody with a wagon on fire.

About the Author

Chris Solaas was born in Memphis, TN in 1963, the fourth child in a happy Norwegian/Italian family. He began writing stories at the tender age of 8. Many years later he began writing songs and poems and short stories.

He graduated from the University of Memphis in Electrical Engineering, and began a career in Computer Programming. Things don't always work out the way you plan. He still lives in the Greater Memphis area, married to a wonderful wife and with four children of his own.

Chris has quite a few novels, which can be purchased on Amazon, as well as over 100 songs, several of them from this book, and many of which can be downloaded for free on his Soundclick sites.

His writings and musings can be accessed through his blog at: http://www.lynvia.com, and he can be followed on various social media sites like Twitter and Facebook, from links at the top of that site.

If you enjoyed this book, give it a rating and leave a review, and check out his other books at Amazon.com

Made in the USA
Columbia, SC
13 June 2023

17984564R00067